PARADE

BY Alexis Braud

PELICAN PUBLISHING COMPANY
Gretna 2016

The word "Pelican" and the depiction of a pelican are trademarks of Pelican Publishing Company, Inc., and are registered in the U.S. Patent and Trademark Office.

ISBN 9781455621484
E-book 9781455621491

Printed in Malaysia
Published by Pelican Publishing Company, Inc.
1000 Burmaster Street, Gretna, Louisiana 70053

*To Sue, for keeping the faith, to Paul for believing,
and to Anorah, Owen and Edgar, just because.*

On a fine misty morning, a small little mouse
woke up in the garden by his little house.

He didn't want cheese, or cool lemonade.
That mouse, well he wanted to lead a parade.

So, he did.

With his little flag flying, he strolled down the walk, and a tabby cat followed in a curious stalk.

Before the cat could decide to jump or to pounce,
he picked up the groove and fell in with a bounce.
If ya can't eat 'em, join 'em!

Two fluffy dogs were all sniffing about
and saw the strange pair all hanging out.

Nothing to chew and nothing to lose,
so they joined in the line to get down
with the blues.
Well, the beat anyway.

Squirrels heard the ruckus from up in their branches,
and decided that fun was worth taking some chances.

They scurried and fell in with small furry feet.
They moved and they chattered along with the beat.
Who knew squirrels could dance?

Raccoons were scrounging a snack then peeked out
to see what the sidewalk was buzzing about.

A few tambourines and what do ya know?
A cool bandit pair was off stealing the show.
Love the colors!

Next to join in was a fox with some brass.

Then a goat with a tuba.

And a pig with some sass.

Then a small troupe of rats all done up for a fete twirled in a row and all played clarinet.
Ya dig?

High-stepping egrets crested and proud and some crows in fine hats fluttered into the crowd.

Feathers all colored and eyes all so bright, this parade might last all afternoon into the night.

Or into tomorrow!

A big mama possum, with babes on her back,
swaggered into the line with a hey and a clap.

Next to join were a couple of friendly alligators in fine evening outfits best meant for head waiters.

From the cafe came pigeons, gray wings all a-flapping.
They perched on the tuba, and then just started napping.

A pelican swooped in and took up a seat on a cart whose mule was clip-clopping his feet.

The cart soon filled up
with a load of fine critters.

Each wearing their best,
all with sparkles and glitter.

From the mouse to the donkey, it was so hard to see
which critter was feeling more fine—or more free.

They shuffled and padded.
They squawked and they stomped.
Round and round the whole square they twirled and they romped.

And when they were worn out, well what do you think?

They did what most do . . .they all stopped for a drink!

Author's Note

Many things are special about the place that I come from.

South Louisiana has incredible people and a diverse gumbo of cultures creating music, cuisine, architecture, and events that are unique on a global scale.

One feature of many of our celebrations, happy or sad, sacred or secular, is parading.

From the complex Mardi Gras to the simple walking krewe, all you need is a stretch of road, a few friends, and a notion to get out and show your stuff for all to see.

Parade was written to capture the spontaneous joy of stepping out.

—Alexis Braud